DETECTIVE DUCK

DUCK

BOOK 2

DETECTIVE DUCK

AMULET BOOKS • NEW YORK

Cataloging-in-Publication Data has been applied for and may be obtained from the Library of Congress.

ISBN 978-1-4197-6681-7

Text © 2024 Henry Winkler and Lin Oliver
Illustrations © 2024 Dan Santat
Book design by Deena Micah Fleming

Printed and bound in China
10 9 8 7 6 5 4 3 2 1

Amulet Books are available at special discounts when purchased in quantity for premiums and promotions as well as fundraising or educational use. Special editions can also be created to specification. For details, contact specialsales@abramsbooks.com or the address below.

ABRAMS The Art of Books
195 Broadway, New York, NY 10007
abramsbooks.com

To all the children on the earth who care about our planet. And to Stacey, always.
—H.W.

With love to the wonderful Waxman next gen: Lyle, Charlie, and Fen.
—L.O.

For the PBG.
—D.S.

CHAPTER 1

The sun was shining and the breeze was blowing over Dogwood Pond. As the dragonflies buzzed and the fish swam slowly along the bank, life seemed peaceful and calm. But it wasn't. Franny the frog was in a panic, her little frog heart pounding in her green-spotted chest. She hopped out of the water like she was being chased by a mean weasel—which, in fact, she was!

Snout, the no-good weasel, flashed his sharp teeth at Franny. He backed her up against a thick pine tree and leaned his snarling face so close, she could feel his hot breath.

"I want breakfast," he growled.

"Well, I'm not available," she said bravely.

"I don't like frogs for breakfast anyway," Snout snapped. "I want you to make me breakfast at your lily pad café. A big order of Franny's fried flies with a side of stewed mosquitoes."

"The café is closed for an emergency," Franny said. "My son, Tad the tadpole, is missing. I have to find Willow. She's a detective. She'll know what to do."

"Ha!" Snout snickered. "That little duck just *thinks* she's a detective. She doesn't have a clue."

"She'll find *all* the clues," Franny said. "If anyone can find my son, it's Willow."

"Did someone say my name?" quacked a nearby voice.

It was Willow, waddling on her webbed feet down the path to the pond. She was wearing a necklace made from the green leaves she had gathered from the grove of willow trees. Her father, Beaver McBeaver, had named her after those beautiful trees. Willow felt lucky her egg had floated downstream and landed in his dam. She had hatched there, and Beaver McBeaver had raised her with all his love.

"Willow!" Franny said. "Thank goodness you're here. Tad is missing. I'm so worried something terrible has happened to him."

Willow gave Snout a suspicious look. "Did you hurt Tad, you evil weasel?"

"Why would I mess with a little squirt like him?"
Snout said with a laugh. "He's so small, he wouldn't
even make a whole snack."

Willow tapped her webbed foot, as she always did when she was thinking.

"Maybe Tad's under a lily pad," Willow said. "Every time my head is underwater, I notice him playing hide-and-seek in the roots."

"I've checked," Franny said. "He's not there. Snout, you better not have hurt him."

"I wasn't even in the pond," Snout said.

"I believe he's telling the truth," Willow said with a nod.

"How do you know?" Franny asked.

"His feet are dry," Willow pointed out. "If he had been chasing Tad in the pond, his fur would be dripping wet. Poof! Mystery solved."

"No, it's not," Franny said. "We still haven't found Tad."

"Those humans probably caught him," Snout said. "I saw one a few minutes ago at the other end of the pond."

"A human! Oh no!" Franny started to cry, her bulging frog eyes filling with tears. "My poor baby tadpole captured by humans."

"Try to stay calm," Willow said, giving Franny a hug with her fluffy wings. "I will help you find him."

"Find who?" came a voice from the nearby mud puddle. It was Sal, the yellow-spotted salamander who was Willow's best friend. He was holding a torn page from a wet comic book he had found on the grassy bank. Sal loved to read comic book adventures, especially when they were soggy.

"Tad is missing," Willow explained.

"Oh, I bet he got zapped by Electro-Man and transformed into a giant squid who lives in a crystal cave at the bottom of the pond."

"Sal, there you go again," Willow said. "Life at Dogwood Pond isn't a comic book."

"Says who?" Sal went on. "I bet the giant squid grew tentacles of steel and dug a trench all the way to China."

"Oh, no," Franny cried. "Don't tell me my son is in China. How will I ever find him there?"

"Whoa, slow down, everyone," Willow said. "Detectives can't make up stories. We have to gather clues. Let me call my clue-gathering team."

Willow let out a long, low honk. Her father, Beaver McBeaver, heard the danger call and came swimming over, paddling with his big, flat tail.

"What do you need, my darling duckling?" he asked, pulling a twig from in between his big beaver teeth. "I'm working on dam repairs."

"I need clues, Dad," Willow said. "Can you swim around the whole pond and see if you can find Tad? He's missing."

"Consider it done," her father answered, doing a flip turn and swimming off.

Flitter, who was playing tag with her dragonfly pals, had also heard the call and came buzzing over.

"What's up?" she asked.

"I need your gigantic dragonfly eyeballs," Willow said.

"You can't have them," Flitter answered. "They're attached."

"I mean I need you to use them. Fly high over the pond and see if you can spot Tad."

"Hurry," Franny added. "He could be on his way to China."

"And if you see Electro-Man, would you get his autograph for me?" Sal shouted as Flitter took off into the air.

The search for Tad was on! Flitter zoomed into the sky to circle the pond while Beaver McBeaver swam the banks.

"Now what do we do?" Franny croaked.

"Now we wait," Willow said, tapping her webbed foot. "The clues will tell us what to do next."

CHAPTER 2

It didn't take long for Flitter to spot the first clue. A human boy was kneeling at the pond's edge, right where the metal pipe carried brown water from the fields into the pond. The boy was splashing in the water, trying to race leaves as if they were little boats. He was having fun until his glasses slipped off his nose and fell into the pond.

"Oh no!" he cried.

Flitter had never seen human glasses before. She knew they must be important, because the boy flung himself onto his stomach and tried to grab them from the water. He missed. Flitter didn't have time to stay and watch him splash around in the pond. She was on a mission to find Tad. *Perhaps he's taking a mud bath over by the dogwood trees*, she thought.

As Flitter zoomed off, the boy's glasses slowly sank below the water's surface. They floated down, down, down into the reeds, where Harry the catfish was napping.

Plop! The glasses landed smack on Harry's nose and woke him up!

"Hey, what's going on?" Harry said, opening his eyes and looking around. He was both frightened and thrilled. "I can see!" he shouted. "Everything is suddenly so clear! Look at the reeds. They look like horse's tails. I never noticed that before. And all those water fleas! Who knew there were so many of them? No wonder I itch under my fins."

Harry swam around the pond, looking through the glasses at all the little things he had never noticed before—tiny crayfish, turtle eggs, goose feathers, even pond scum.

"This pond is a mess," he grumbled. "Somebody needs to do a better job cleaning. Not me, of course, but somebody."

Suddenly, a huge brown shape appeared before him. It surprised him so much, he belched bubbles. "Get out of my way. This is my part of the pond!" he snapped. "What are you, anyway? A bear? If so, I hope you've already eaten lunch."

"It's just me, Harry," Beaver McBeaver said. "You've seen me every day of your life."

"You look different," Harry said. "I never knew you had orange teeth. You should brush those things."

"Don't talk to me about my dental habits," Beaver McBeaver said. "Your breath smells like old turtle poop. And by the way, what are those round things on your face?"

"I don't know. They just fell out of the sky," Harry said. "But my eyes love them. I can see things I've never seen before."

"That's good news," Beaver said, "because I'm looking for Tad. He's gone missing."

"Kids!" Harry said, shaking his head. "You can't keep track of them. That really prickles my scales."

"Do you think you could help me find him?" Beaver asked.

"I was just taking a nap. Could you come back in half an hour?"

"No, this is urgent. Everyone is worried and we need to find Tad now."

"Okay." Harry sighed. "Maybe I can find him with my new magic eyes. Come on, let's get on with it."

Together, they swam along the banks, looking under mossy stones and lily pad roots, but there was no sign of Tad. As they swam past the metal pipe, the pond water seemed to change color. It became a strange shade of blue.

"My new eyes really are magic," Harry said. "Everything is turning blue. Even these plants all around us are blue."

"More like blue-green," Beaver McBeaver said.

"And did you notice it's kind of hard to take a deep breath?" Harry asked. "My gills are stuffy."

"Yes, I'm feeling that too." Beaver McBeaver nodded. "Not in my gills, of course, but in my nose."

Beaver McBeaver and Harry had entered a part of their pond filled with blue-green algae. The plants were so thick, Beaver and Harry could barely see through them.

"That's odd," Harry said. "I've never noticed these blue-green plants before."

"You've never noticed them because they weren't here," Beaver McBeaver said. "Something is wrong. Plants shouldn't be this thick. And they shouldn't be bright blue."

"What do you have against blue?" Harry grumbled. "The sky is blue and you don't have a problem with that."

"Blue things don't live in ponds," Beaver McBeaver said.

"Flitter's wings are blue," said Harry. "And she lives by the pond."

"But not *in* it," Beaver McBeaver answered. "Not like you and me."

"Or like that frog over there hiding in the reeds," Harry added.

Beaver McBeaver looked over and saw a little green frog hanging on to a single stalk of reed. He was wiggling like a worm.

"Look at that little guy," Beaver said to Harry.

"He looks like he's trying to dance."

"You call that dancing? No way," Harry said. "That frog could stand to learn a few of my smooth dance moves."

"What dance moves? You don't even have feet," Beaver said.

"Well, these fins can really shake it up. Just ask Iris, the smallmouth bass who lives upstream. My dance moves had her blowing bubbles for weeks."

"Did you notice that frog has only three legs?" Beaver asked Harry.

"Sure, I can see everything, even those little red spots on his back. There are three of them and they make a square."

"That's not a square, Harry. That's a triangle. Three makes a triangle."

"Hey, give me a break. I'm a fish."

From above the pond came the muffled sound of a long, low honk.

"That's Willow, calling me back," Beaver McBeaver said. "Maybe she has some news about Tad. I better hurry."

"Can I come with you?" Harry asked. "I can't wait to show everyone my new magic eyes."

"Sure, just swim behind me," Beaver answered. "If you get too close, your breath will curl my nose hairs."

"Nose hairs! I don't have those," Harry said. "Can I see yours close-up?"

"I'm going to pretend you didn't say that,"

Beaver said, groaning. "Now, let's hurry. Willow is waiting and Tad is still out there somewhere."

As they swam to meet Willow, they saw Flitter zooming in from the dogwood trees. She had heard Willow's call too and was speeding back to report her news. Willow was waiting on the bank, pacing up and down, with Sal on her back and Franny hopping beside her.

"What did you find?" Willow asked before Beaver and Flitter had even reached her.

"Did you see Tad?" Franny added quickly. "Please tell me you found him."

Beaver McBeaver took a long breath. He knew what it was like to worry about a child. He had often worried about Willow when she was little. The pond could be a dangerous place for a baby duckling.

Now he was going to have to find a way to break the sad news to Franny. There was no sign of Tad. They had seen many things on their search, but not one of them was a little tadpole.

CHAPTER 3

Beaver McBeaver, Flitter, and Harry were all talking at once. Willow tried to listen carefully, but it wasn't easy.

"We saw a human boy," Flitter buzzed, "who had magic eyes, but then he lost them in the water and they sank all the way down."

"And they landed on my nose," Harry added.

"Yes, I see that," Willow said. "You have to give them back, Harry. They don't belong to you."

"Finders keepers," Harry said. "Besides, they make me see great. When I look through them, I can see every little thing, even your father's nose hairs, which, by the way, aren't that little."

"Forget my nose hairs," Beaver McBeaver snapped. "Tell them about the three-legged frog we saw, doing a wild and crazy dance."

"Some dancing," Harry said. "It looked like he had ants in his pants."

"How does any of this chatter help us find Tad?" Franny groaned. "We're wasting time here and my little guy could be in terrible danger."

Willow had been tapping her feet while she listened. First her left foot and then her right foot. That's what she did when her detective brain was working super hard.

"Wait just a minute, Franny," she said. "An idea is coming to me."

"I think I see a light bulb turning on over your head," Sal said to Willow. "It's just like when Doctor Brain figures out that Elastic Man isn't really elastic but is made of mashed potatoes."

"Stop the comic book talk, Sal," Willow said. "I'm making a mental list of questions to help me sort out the clues."

"This sounds important," Sal said. "Everyone, fire up your brains."

"Question number one," Willow said. "Flitter, you saw the human boy. Where exactly was he? Question two: Harry, you were looking through magic eyes. Did you see anything unusual? Three: Dad, you saw a three-legged frog? Did you notice any details about him? Flitter, you go first. And no one interrupt her, please."

Flitter cleared her little dragonfly throat.

"The boy was at the far end of the bank," she said, "where the metal pipe dumps that brown water into our pond."

"And that's right where I saw the underwater forest of blue-green plants," Harry added. "They were so thick, we could hardly swim or breathe."

"Hmm," Willow said. "That doesn't sound good."

"And what I noticed," Beaver McBeaver chimed in, "was that the three-legged frog was on a reed that was growing right next to those blue-green plants."

"That's the answer!" cried Sal. "Those plants are from outer space. The frog ate them and turned into a three-legged mutant. Makes perfect sense."

Willow shook her head. "It's an interesting theory, Sal," she said, "but you don't really have any clues to back it up. Detectives have to depend on facts."

"Well, here's a fact," said Beaver McBeaver. "That frog had a little bump where his fourth leg should have been. And three red spots on his back in the shape of a triangle."

Willow's eyes lit up. She turned to Franny. "Does Tad have any red spots on his back?" she asked.

"Yes, he does!" Franny answered. "Three red ones."

"Are they shaped like a triangle?" Willow asked, her heart starting to beat faster.

"Yes, they are," Franny said. "Just like his father's."

"Poof," Willow said. "Mystery solved. That little frog was Tad!"

"But he's a tadpole, not a frog," Franny said.

"He *was* a tadpole," Willow said. "My dad and Harry were looking right at Tad without even knowing it. Tad the tadpole was in the process of changing into Tad the frog."

"But he wasn't supposed to grow into a frog until next month," Franny said. "I have it marked on my lily pad calendar."

"Nature moves at its own pace," Willow said. "I wonder if that new blue-green algae has anything to do with this?"

"Or all that brown water from the pipe?" Flitter asked.

"Hmmm, these are interesting facts," Willow said, tapping her foot again.

"We don't have time for interesting facts!" Franny croaked. "We have to find Tad. Fast!"

"Great!" Sal said. "I love a rescue mission. Let's go!"

Sal jumped on Willow's back and grabbed her fluffy yellow feathers like he was riding a pony.

"I want to come too," Franny said.

"It's better if you stay here," Willow told her, "just in case Tad swims this way. Dad and Harry, can you lead us to Tad?"

"Sure," Harry said. "Just follow my stinky smell."

"For once, it comes in handy," Sal muttered.

As they set out across the pond, paddling at top speed, Aaron the heron flew by overhead. When Willow saw him, she let out her long, low emergency honk.

"Helloooo down there," he called to his pals. "What's the problem?"

"We're looking for Tad," Willow called. "Can you join our search party?"

"Sure, I'll cover the airspace," Aaron said.

"Wait a minute, that's my job," said Flitter.

"A search party calls for a large wingspan," Aaron said. "You're too small."

"Small can be mighty," Flitter said. "Just watch me." She shot ahead, doing backflips in the air using only two of her four wings.

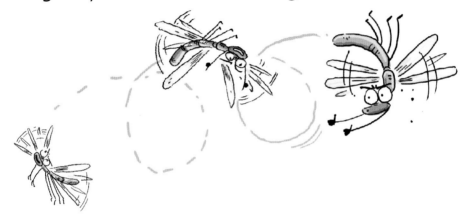

"Show-off," Aaron said under his breath.

"I see the blue-green plant forest," Flitter called back to them. "It's just up ahead."

"I'll dive under the water and look for Tad," Willow said.

"What about me?" Sal asked. "I don't do underwater."

"You can wait here with me," Beaver McBeaver said. "Hop aboard."

He swam up next to Willow. Sal jumped off Willow's back and onto Beaver McBeaver's. It was so slippery that he couldn't get a solid grip.

"Whoa, I'm sliding off and it hurts my tail," he said. "No offense, but your skin is pretty bumpy."

Before Sal could sink below the surface, Beaver McBeaver scooped him up with his tail and flipped him onto his back.

"Hey, that was fun," Sal said. "Can we do that again?"

"No, you can't," Willow said. "We're on a rescue mission. I'm going to bring Tad up. Everyone, wait here. I'll be right back."

"Remember, it's hard to breathe down there," her father warned her.

Willow took a deep breath and ducked under the water, where Harry was waiting for her. The blue-green algae was so thick, it was hard to see. Slowly, Willow and Harry made their way through the dark and cloudy water. They were finding it hard to breathe too. Willow felt dizzy. The blue-green plants were swirling all around her, getting tangled in her webbed feet.

She had always felt right at home in Dogwood Pond, but now the water felt dangerous. Her heart beat fast as she tried to overcome her fear.

"I can do this," she said quietly.

But could she? She wasn't sure.

CHAPTER 4

Willow gathered up her courage.

"I have to face my fear," she told herself. "For Tad's sake."

She and Harry made their way into the thick curtain of swaying algae. They darted this way and that. They were searching for a three-legged frog, but they didn't find one. What they found instead was a four-legged frog hanging on to the reeds.

Willow looked at the little frog. At first, she couldn't believe her eyes. She swam right up to him and stared directly at him. Yes, it was true. That frog had three red spots on its back in the shape of a triangle!

"Tad," Willow quacked, "is that you?"

"Of course it's me," Tad said. "You've known me your whole life."

"But you're a frog. And you have all four legs!"

"Cool, huh?" Tad laughed. "This fourth one just popped out, and I want to tell you, it wasn't easy. I'm so tired, I need to take a nap. So if you'll excuse me, I'd like some privacy."

"As soon as we get back to your mother's lily pad, you can sleep all day long," Harry said.

"My mother?" Tad shook his head. "Not so fast. I'm not going back there."

"But your mother is worried sick about you," Willow told him.

"She misses you and your bony little tail," Harry said.

"I don't have a tail anymore," Tad snapped. "In case you haven't noticed, I'm not a baby tadpole.

I'm a teenage frog. I need my space. A lily pad of my own."

Willow didn't have enough air to argue with Tad and neither did Harry. They were having such a hard time breathing.

"I've got to go get some air," Willow said to Tad. "Promise me you'll wait right here."

"I can't promise you that," Tad said. "I'm a teenager and I was born to run."

"You were born to hop," Harry said. "And I strongly suggest you hop back to your mother."

Willow started to feel so dizzy, she could hardly see. She needed to get air, fast. There wasn't even enough time to convince Tad to come with her. Pointing her bill straight up, she shot through the water until she reached the surface. She sucked in as much air as she could until she no longer felt dizzy.

Harry followed her up to the top. "Are you okay?" he asked. "That was no party for my gills, either. They had to work overtime."

"I'll be okay, for now at least," Willow said. "Where are the others? I don't see them."

Harry looked around with his magic eyes and saw Beaver McBeaver, Sal, and Aaron hiding behind the reeds. Flitter was buzzing right above them. Harry and Willow swam over to them.

"Why are you hiding?" Willow asked their Pond Squad.

"Shhh," said Sal. "You have to whisper."

"Why?"

Sal pointed his little claw down the bank. "The humans are here," he whispered.

"They're looking for the boy's magic eyes," Flitter buzzed. "He dropped them in the water."

"I think they're called glasses," Beaver McBeaver said. "I heard the big man say this is the third time this month the boy has lost his glasses."

"Talk about losing things," Aaron said. "When I was just a little heron, I lost every fish I caught. My mother always said it was because I chewed with my beak open."

Willow looked at the man and the boy kneeling on the bank. The man wore a uniform and a badge. She had seen him before.

"That's the forest ranger," she whispered to the others.

"Maybe he can help us find Tad," Flitter said.

"Oh, I forgot to tell you," Willow said. "We already found Tad."

Sal squinted his beady eyes and looked around. "Funny, I don't see him. Maybe Captain Doom zapped him with an electron ray and he became invisible. I can see it now: *The Adventures of Invisa-Frog.*"

"Tad's not invisible, Sal." Willow sighed. "He's just stubborn."

"He says he's a teenager now and can do whatever he wants," Harry added.

"His attitude is making me so quacking mad," Willow said. "He just wants to get his own way."

"Don't be so hard on him, my darling duckling," Beaver McBeaver said. "Remember when you moved out of our dam?"

"I had to," Willow said. "I got too big and all your twigs kept poking me in my tail feathers."

"So you packed your things in your Stuff Box and marched off," her father recalled. "You didn't even make it to the big pine tree. You had to yell for me to help you carry your stuff."

"That's different. Tad is being so—"

"Dad!" A human voice interrupted their conversation. It was the boy, who had picked up a slimy piece of the blue-green plant floating in their pond. He held out his hand. "Look at this. It's disgusting."

The ranger glanced at the plant in his son's hand.

"Oh no," he said. "That's blue-green algae. I hope there isn't more growing here. These plants can take over a pond and wipe out everything. They make it hard for the fish and plant life to breathe."

From behind the reeds, Willow and her friends listened intently.

"That's exactly what's happening to our pond," Willow said. "Harry, all that algae is taking over. That's why we couldn't breathe. We have to let the ranger know the algae is spreading."

"How are you going to do that?" Aaron asked, pulling one of his skinny legs up and tucking it under his wing.

"Detective Duck to the rescue," Willow said. "I'm going over there."

"To the humans?" Beaver McBeaver said. "That's dangerous."

"Not as dangerous as losing our pond," Willow said.

She took a deep breath to gather her confidence and then swam off. She had only gone a few feet when she turned around and swam right back.

"I knew this would happen," said Sal. "You

realized you need me for backup."

"You?" Flitter said. "What can you do?"

"Not much, but I'm handsome," Sal said.

Willow swam up to Harry, opened her bill, and plucked the boy's glasses off his face.

"Hey," Harry complained. "Those are my magic eyes. What are you doing?"

"Returning them," Willow said. "They're not yours."

"But I love them," Harry protested.

"So does that little boy," she said. "And he needs them to see."

With the glasses firmly in her bill and bravery in her heart, Willow swam off to face the humans.

CHAPTER 5

Willow made her way across the pond to the metal pipe and then stopped. As she bobbed up and down, she saw the brown mucky water pouring into the pond. Even though the man and the boy were standing nearby, they didn't notice her or the brown water flowing from the pipe.

Hmmm . . . she thought. *I need to get their attention. But how? If I honk, I'll open my bill and the glasses will fall into the water and sink.*

Willow's detective brain thought hard. She tried to tap her foot as she always did when she was solving a case, but there was no ground underneath. When she tapped, she just splashed water into her

eyes. But as always, she still came up with a great idea.

What if I use the glasses to tap on the metal pipe? she wondered. *The humans will notice the noise and look my way. They'll see me and this awful dirty water. Poof, mystery solved!*

Gently, she tapped one end of the glasses on the pipe. It made a clinking sound as the frame hit the metal. She watched the humans, but they didn't look over, so she tried again.

Clink, clink, clink.

Nothing. She hit the pipe a little harder.

Clank, clank, CLANK!

This time it worked. The man and the boy turned their heads and looked directly at her.

"Dad, I can't believe it!" the boy said. "That little duck has my glasses. Do you think she knows they're mine?"

"Animals know more than we think," his father replied. "Look what else she's showing us. That pipe."

"Why is the pipe there?" the boy asked.

"It's draining the runoff water from the farms that surround the pond," his father explained.

"Is it bad for the pond?"

"Often, runoff water is full of chemicals, like pesticides and fertilizers. Wait a minute. I bet those chemicals are causing all that blue-green algae to bloom and invade the pond."

"That's terrible," the boy said. "Can we fix it, Dad?"

"I'm going to try," the ranger said. "I'll have to talk to the farmers about keeping their runoff water out of this pond. And ask them not to use dangerous chemicals in their fields."

Those words were like music to Willow's ears. The ranger was going to help them solve the problem! The brown water would go away! And then the blue-green algae would too! They would be able to breathe underwater again, and Dogwood Pond would return to its natural beauty.

These humans weren't there to hurt them. They were there to help.

If ducks could hug, Willow would have given the ranger the biggest hug ever. Instead, she kicked her webbed feet, flapped her wings, and swam to the bank. She waddled up to the humans, opened her bill, and dropped the glasses right at the boy's feet.

Before the boy could bend down to pick them up, a black furry tail darted from the reeds and grabbed the glasses. The tail was attached to none other than that no-good weasel, Snout.

"Hey, Snout," Willow quacked. "Give those back."

"In your dreams. They're mine now," Snout growled, running off into the grove of dogwood trees.

"Not if I have anything to say about it!" Willow said, taking off after him.

Weasels are faster than ducks, and Willow knew she needed help to catch Snout. She let out her long, low emergency honk, hoping her Pond Squad would hear her. Then she took off into the air, flying low along the ground, following Snout as he ran. He was quick, weaving in and out of trees and hiding behind rocks.

"Can't catch me, you web-footed slowpoke," he yelled.

He wasn't counting on the pond pals joining the chase. When he looked up ahead, he was surprised to see a big problem on the path. A problem in the shape of a beaver.

"Uh-oh," he said.

Beaver McBeaver stood on his hind legs, balancing his huge body on his tail. He flashed his big orange teeth at Snout.

"Going someplace?" he asked.

Snout looked up to the sky and saw Aaron the heron circling overhead. Before Snout could duck for cover, Aaron swooped down and pecked him on the head with his long, sharp beak. Flitter swooped down too, buzzing in and out of Snout's ears. Sal was cheerleading from a nearby rock.

"We've got you surrounded, you stealing weasel," Sal shouted. "You're trapped like a fly in Spider-Woman's web!"

"I'm just itching to give you another peck on the head," Aaron called from above.

"I'm going to buzz in your ears," Flitter yelled. "I'm small, but annoying!"

Snout covered his head and his ears, trying to hide.

"He's all yours," Sal said. "Go for it, Willow!"

Willow pounced on Snout from behind and grabbed his tail in her bill. Snout tried to run, but she held him so tightly, he couldn't escape. With

his legs spinning around and around, he looked like a rat on a treadmill.

"Let go of my tail," shouted Snout.

"She will when you drop the glasses, punk," Sal yelled.

Willow clamped her bill down even harder.

"Ow! That hurts!" Snout cried. He looked up and saw Aaron coming in for another peck. Flitter buzzed under his nostrils, making him feel like he had to sneeze.

"You can end it all now," Sal said. "Just say the word."

"Okay, okay, I give up," Snout whimpered. He dropped the glasses onto the ground in front of him. Willow let go of his tail and grabbed the glasses in her bill. And before she could say, "Scat, you weaselly weasel," Snout was off and running into the woods like a rocket heading for the moon.

The boy and his father had caught up to Willow and watched the whole fight. They'd seen the animals surround Snout. They'd seen Willow hold him by the tail. They'd heard Snout whimper and seen him drop the glasses and run. They couldn't believe it!

"Dad, that little duck is amazing!" the boy said.

Willow fluffed up her feathers and picked up the boy's glasses in her bill. Sticking her chest out as far as it would go, she marched over to the boy and dropped the glasses at his feet again. She let out a quack as if to say, *You better hold on to these from now on, kiddo.*

"You must be the smartest duck I've ever met," the ranger said. "It's going to make me very happy to save your pond."

"Can I help save the pond too?" the boy asked.

"We all can," his father answered. "Keeping our waters clean is everyone's responsibility. Isn't that right, little duck?"

Willow flapped her wings. Flitter and Aaron flapped theirs, too. Sal clapped his claws, and Beaver McBeaver slapped his tail on the ground. From the pond, even grumpy Harry wiggled his fins. The boy and his father put their arms in the air and cheered.

It was great to see the humans and the animals all celebrating how working together will save Dogwood Pond.

CHAPTER 6

Later that day, Willow and her friends were gathered at Franny's Café. Franny was whipping up some fried mosquito wings with a side of flies.

"I can't believe my little Tad is a frog now," Franny said. "I miss him, but at least I know he's safe."

"He'll come back, you wait and see," Beaver McBeaver said. "He just needs a little time to grow up."

"What I actually need is a big order of stewed mosquito wings and fried flies," croaked a voice from the next lily pad.

The animals spun around and there was Tad, a

big grin across his new frog face.

"You're back!" Franny screamed, jumping onto her son's lily pad and throwing her webbed feet around him. "And look at you. So handsome. And so tall."

"And so hungry," Tad said.

"It's good to see you, kid," said Sal.

"Thanks. I'm looking pretty cool, don't you think?"

"Listen to him," Harry said. "He thinks he's a big shot just because he has all four legs now."

"You know, Taddy, you're always welcome to come back here," Franny said. "There's a nice empty lily pad next to mine. You'd have your own place but still be close to all of us."

"Actually," Tad said, "I've been thinking about that. Turns out the place I picked at the other end of the pond is pretty noisy. There are lots of humans gathered around, talking like crazy."

"What are they saying?" Flitter asked.

"Lots of stuff," Tad said. "Like how they're going to talk to the farmers about what chemicals they use. And how they're going to remove that brown water pipe. And get rid of the blue-green algae, whatever that is."

"Those are all great things to talk about," Willow said.

"Unless you're trying to sleep," Tad answered.

"It's nice and quiet here," Flitter said. "You could move back."

"And stay here forever," Aaron said. "With all your friends."

"Where the flies are crunchy and the mosquito wings are juicy," his mother added.

"How can a frog say no to mosquito wings?" Tad said. "It's a deal. From now on, my old home is my new home!"

"Oh, Taddy!" Franny cried, reaching out to give him a sticky frog kiss.

"Uh, no more Taddy, Mom," Tad said. "Tad is my grown-up name. And easy on the smooches. I'm a teenager now."

They all laughed and helped themselves to Franny's delicious food. At the other end of the pond, the humans were busy creating plans to make Dogwood Pond healthy again. Little did they know that the buzzing and quacking and croaking

they heard in the distance were the sounds of Willow and her friends celebrating Tad's return.

Willow looked around at her wonderful friends and her beautiful pond, safe once again.

Poof, she thought. *Problem solved.*

ACKNOWLEDGMENTS

It takes a lot of talented people to hatch a duck detective, and we are so grateful for our team of talented people who brought our pond squad into the childen's book world.

Thank you to our publisher, Andrew Smith, who said yes to the duck; and to our editor, Maggie Lehrman, who guides us through the process with skill and care. And to Mary Marolla, who makes traveling for the duck such a pleasure, all our gratitude.

There are no words to express our admiration for the talented Dan Santat, whose illustrations make our characters so lively and lovable. Dan, what you bring to this series is pure joy.

Our agents, Esther Newberg and Ellen Goldsmith-Vein, have provided support and guidance through all our literary endeavors. This book, and many others, wouldn't be here without them.

We want to extend our hopes and dreams for a healthy future for our world to all the kids who might read this book. We hope you learn to love the natural world so you can protect it always.

—Henry Winkler and Lin Oliver

ABOUT THE AUTHORS

Henry Winkler is an Emmy Award–winning actor, writer, director, and producer who has created some of the most iconic TV roles, including Arthur "the Fonz" Fonzarelli on *Happy Days* and Gene Cousineau on *Barry*.

Lin Oliver is a children's book writer and a writer and producer for both TV and film. She is the cofounder of the Society for Children's Book Writers and Illustrators (SCBWI) and is the managing director of the SCBWI Impact and Legacy Fund.

ABOUT THE ILLUSTRATOR

Dan Santat is the *New York Times* bestselling author of over one hundred books for children, including *Are We There Yet?*, *After The Fall*, and *The Adventures of Beekle: The Unimaginary Friend*, for which he won the Caldecott Medal. He lives in Southern California with his wife, two kids, and many, many pets.

STAY TUNED FOR THE NEXT

DETECTIVE DUCK

MYSTERY!

AND CATCH UP WITH BOOK ONE!

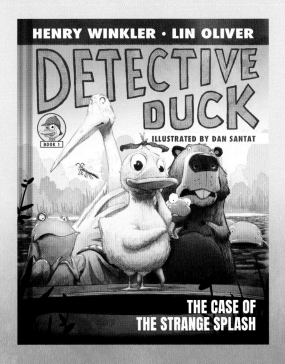

HENRY WINKLER · LIN OLIVER

DETECTIVE DUCK

BOOK 1

ILLUSTRATED BY DAN SANTAT

THE CASE OF
THE STRANGE SPLASH